PEACEMAKER

PEACEMAKER

by Alan E. Nourse

Flicker's mind fought silently and desperately to maintain its fast-receding control, to master his frantic urge to writhe and scream in agony at the burning light. The fetid animal stench of the aliens filled his nostrils, gagging him; the heat of the place seared his skin like a thousand white-hot needles, and seeped into his throat to blister his lungs. It didn't matter that his arms and legs were bound tightly to the pallet, for he knew he dared not move them. The maddening off-and-on of the scorching light set his mind afire, twisted his stomach into a hard knot of fear and agony, but his body lay still as death, relaxed and motionless. He knew that the instant he betrayed his' tortured alertness by so much as a single tremor, his chance for contact would be totally gone.

"The only sensible thing to do is to kill it!"

It was not repetition but a constant, powerful force, crashing into his mind, hateful, cold. He heard no sound but the muffled throb of spaceship engines far back in the ship, but the *thought* was there, adamant and uncompromising. It burst from the garbled, thought-patterns of the others and struck his mind like an electric shock. One of the aliens wanted to kill him.

Thought contact. It was a paralyzing concept to Flicker. The aliens couldn't possibly realize it themselves; they were using sound communication with one another, on a sonic level beyond the sensitivity of Flicker's ears. He could hear no sound—but the thought patterns that guided the sound-talking of the aliens came through to sledge-hammer his brain, coherent, crystal clear.

*

"But why kill it? We have it sedated almost to death-level now. It's completely unconscious, it's securely bound, and we can keep it that way until we reach home. Then it's no longer our worry."

The first thought broke out again with new overtones of anger and fear. "I say we've got to kill it! We had no right picking it up in the first place. What is it? How did it get there? Where was the ship that

5

brought it?" The alien mind was venomous. "Kill it now, while we can!"

Flicker tried desperately to tear his mind from the agonizing rhythm of the light, to catch and hold the alien thoughts. Confusion rose in his mind, and for the first time he felt a chill of fear. His people knew that these aliens were avaricious and venal—a dozen drained and pillaged star-systems which they had overrun bore witness to that—but he had never even considered, before he started on this mission, that they might kill him without even attempting communication. Why must they kill him? All he wanted was a chance—one brief moment to convey his message to them. Five years of planning, and his own life, had been risked just to get the message to them, to gain their confidence and make them understand, but all he found in these alien minds was fear and suspicion and hate, which had become a single ever-developing crescendo: "Kill it now, while we can!"

There were only three of them with him now, but he knew, from some corner of the alien minds, that five others were sleeping in a forward chamber of the ship. He saw himself clearly, alone on an unknown spacecraft with eight alien creatures, gliding through interstellar space at unthinkable speed, bound for that nebulous and threatening somewhere they called home. Their home. He caught a brief mind-picture from one of them of an enormous city, teeming with these alien creatures, watching him, picking at him, trying to question him, deciding how to kill him

And through everything else came the intermittent burning glare of that terrible white light—

Then suddenly the three aliens were leaving the cabin. Flicker sensed their indecision, felt them balancing the question in their minds. Soundlessly, he lifted one eyelid a trifle. The searing light burst in on his retina, blinding him for a moment; then he caught a distorted glimpse of them opening the hatch and withdrawing in their jerking, uneven gait. And still the alien thought came through

ALAN E. NOURSE

with a parting jab to his tortured mind: "The only thing we can do is to kill it. The risk of tampering with it is too great. And we don't dare take it back home alive."

The light was gone now. Flicker took a deep breath of the heavy air, allowing his tensed muscles to relax as the sweet coolness and comfort crept through his body. First he stretched his legs, as far as they would go in the restrainers, then his arms, and coughed a time or two to clear his throat. Almost fearfully he opened his eyes to the cool, soothing darkness. His mind still ached with the afterglow of the furious lights, but gradually the details of the cabin appeared. Far in the background the throbbing drive of the great ship altered subtly, then increased slightly in volume. Bound where? Flicker sighed, trying to turn his mind away from the undermining awareness of failure, of something gone very wrong. Carefully he reviewed his rescue, his actions, the aliens' reactions. They had cut their drive almost immediately when they had spotted him, and sent out a lifeboat for him without previous reconnaissance ; surely he had been helpless enough when they dragged him from his crippled *gig*, half-frozen, to allay any suspicions of his immediate dangerousness. A crippled man is no menace, nor an exhausted man. The whole thing had been carefully planned and skillfully executed. The aliens couldn't have detected his own ship which had dropped him off hours before, in the proper place to intercept their ship. And yet they were suspicious and fearful, as well as curious, and their first thought was to kill him first, and examine him after he was dead.

Flicker's face twisted into a sour grin at the irony. To think that he had come, so quietly and naively, to these aliens as a peacemaker! If he were killed, the loss would be theirs far more than his. Because contact, living contact, and a mutual meeting of minds was desperately necessary. They had to be warned. For three decades they had been observed, without contact, in their slow, consuming march across the galaxy, conquering, enslaving, pillaging. The curiosity of their nature had started them on their way; greed and lust for power

7

had carried them on until now, at last, they were coming too close. They could not be allowed to come closer. They had to be warned away.

Flicker had been present at the meeting where that decision had been reached. There had been voices raised in favor of attacking the encroaching aliens, without warning, to deal them a crippling blow and send them reeling back home. But most of the leaders had opposed this, and Flicker could see their point. He knew that his people's struggle for peace and security and economic balance had been exhausting, the final settlement dearly won. Part of the utter distaste of his people for outside contact lay deep within Flicker's own mind: they asked no homage from anyone, they desired no power, they felt no need for expansion. The years of war had left them exhausted and peace-hungry, and they demanded but one thing from any culture approaching them: they wanted to be left alone. Cultural and economic contacts they would eagerly seek with this alien race, but they would tolerate no upset diplomatic relations, no attempts to infiltrate and conquer, no lies and forgeries and socio-economic upheavals. They were tired of all these. They had found their way as a people, and with characteristic independence they wanted to follow it, without interference or advice.

And then the aliens had come. Closer and closer, to the very fringes of their confederation. Like a cancer the aliens came, stealthily, nibbling at the fringes, never quite contacting them, never really annoying them, but preparing little by little for the first small bite. And Flicker knew that they could not be allowed to take that bite, for his people would fight, if necessary, to total extinction for the right to be left alone.

Flicker shifted his weight, and sighed helplessly. The plan of his leaders had been simple. A few individual contacts, to warn the aliens. A few well-planned demonstrations of the horrors they could expect if they would not desist. There were other parts of the galaxy for these aliens to explore, other stars for them to ravage. If they could be made to realize the carnage they were inevitably approaching, the frightful battle they were precipitating, they might gladly settle for cultural and commercial contacts. But first they must be stopped and warned. They must not go any further.

Flicker's mind raced through the plan, the words, carefully imprinted in his mind, the evidence he could present to them.

If only he could have a chance! He felt the dull pain in his stomach—he hadn't been fed since he was brought aboard, and the drug they gave him had drained and exhausted him. At least he would have no more of *that* for another three hours. He sighed quietly, aching for sleep. From the moment the impact of the first dose of drug hit him, he had realized the terrible depths of strength his deception would require. He had been nearly unconscious from exposure in outer space when they had dragged him from his lifeboat into the blazing light of the ship, but the drug had stimulated him to the point of convulsions. An overwhelming dosage for *their* metabolism, no doubt, but it had fallen far short of his sedation threshold, driving his heart into a frenzy of activity as he tried to control his jerking muscles. Still, there would be no more for three hours or so, so he could lie in reasonable comfort, trying to find a solution to the question at hand.

One of them wanted to kill him immediately. That was the one who had poked and probed that first day, tapping his nerves and bones with a little hammer, taking samples of his blood and exhaled breath, opening his eyelid and using that horrid torch that seared his brain like raw fire. The throbbing, intermittent light had begun to bother him as early as that. Either their visual pickup was of extremely low sensitivity, or his own neurovisio pickup had been stepped up to such a degree that what appeared as steady light to them registered on his mind as a rapid and maddening oscillation. But the brilliance and the heat—

His strength was returning slowly after the ordeal. His muscles ached from inactivity, and he began twisting back and forth, testing the limits of his restraints. Each leg could move about four inches back and forth ; 'his right arm seemed tightly secured, but his left—he twisted his wrist back and forth slowly, and suddenly it was free! Unbelieving, Flicker groped for the restrainer. It hung loosely at the side of the pallet, its buckle broken. He moved the arm tentatively, testing the other restrainer, wiping perspiration from his forehead. Finally he lay back, his heart pounding. With one arm free he could free himself completely in a matter of moments. But the aliens mustn't know it, for anything that would startle them or make them suspicious might turn the tide of their indecision instantly, and bring sudden violent, purposeless death.

The arm could be used to keep himself alive—if he had to. The thought of the one alien crept through his mind: the cold, unyielding hate, and the fear. The others were merely curious, and curiosity could be his weapon, to help him establish the link that was so necessary. Somehow, contact must be established without frightening them, or threatening them in any way. Although their thoughts came to him so clearly, he had tried in vain to establish mental rapport with them. They showed no sign of awareness of anything but their own thoughts, and communicated only by sound, for their thinking processes were as sluggish as their motions. Sluggish thinking, but on a high level: they thought logically, using data in most cases to form logical, sound conclusions. They understood friendliness, and affection, and companionship, among themselves, but toward him—they seemed unable to conceive of him except in terms of alien, to be feared, investigated, attacked.

He sighed again and settled back, trying to ease his aching back and shoulders. His mind was almost giddy from lack of sleep, running off into wild, dreamlike ramblings, but he struggled for control, fighting to keep the fingers of sleep from his mind. He knew that to sleep now would be to place himself at a terrible, possibly fatal, disadvantage. He couldn't afford to sleep now—not until contact had been established.

The light flashed on again, directly above him. Flicker cringed, his muscles twitching, tightening before the torturous heat. Anger and frustration crept through to his consciousness—why so soon? No more drug was due for a long while yet. He heard footsteps in the passageway outside, and the hatch squeaked open admit one of the aliens, alone. And with him came a single paralyzing thought wave which tore into Flicker's brain, driving out the pain and frustration, leaving nothing but cold fear:

"If the others find it dead, they can't do much about it—"

This, then, was the one that had wanted him dead. They called him Klock, and he was the biggest alien on the crew. This one especially was afraid of him, wanted him dead immediately, and had come to see that he was dead! Alone, on his own initiative, against the will of the others. And in a cold wave of fear, Flicker knew that he would do it.

There was no curiosity in the assassin's mind, only fear and hate. Through one not-quite closed eye Flicker watched the alien approach. It held a syringe-like instrument in its claws, and the oily skin was oozing a foul-smelling fluid that stood in droplets all over its face. The fear in the alien's mind intensified, impinging on Flicker's brain with the drive and force of a trip-hammer, clear and cold. "If the others find it dead, there is nothing they can do—"

The alien was beside him, its head near Flicker's face, and he caught the bright glint of glass and steel, too near. Like lightning Flicker swung with his free arm, a sudden, crushing blow. The alien emitted one small, audible squeak, and dropped to the floor, its thin skull squashed like an eggshell right down to its neck.

Frantic with the maddening light and heat, Flicker ripped away the restraints on his other arm and legs. Ripping a magna-boot from the alien's foot, he heaved it with all his might at the source of the light. There was a loud pop, and the cabin sank into darkness again. Flicker wiped the moisture from his forehead, and stood numb and panting at the side of the table as the afterglow faded and the wonderful

11

coolness crept through him again. And then he saw, almost with a start, the body on the metal floor before him.

Gagging from the stench of the thing, he knelt beside it and examined it with trembling fingers. With the light gone, the alien *had* changed color, its leathery skin now a pasty white, its shaggy mane brown. White stuff oozed from its macerated head, mingled with a red fluid which resembled blood. Flicker dabbed his finger in it, sniffed it. A red body fluid should mean an oxygen metabolism, like his own, but he had concluded from the heavy atmosphere that the aliens were nitrogen-metabolistic. That would account, in part, for their sluggishness, their slow thinking.

Realization of the situation began to crowd into his brain. This creature was dead! He had killed it. He sat back on the floor, panting, trying to channel his wheeling thoughts into a coherent pattern. He'd killed one of the aliens ; that meant that his last hope for peaceful contact was gone. The mission was lost, and his danger critical. Even if he could succeed in concealing himself, it was unthinkable to go with them to their home planet. Escape? Equally unthinkable. They were vengeful creatures, as well as 'curious. Their vengeance might be murderous—

Briefly his wife and family flashed through his mind, waiting for him, so proud that he had been chosen for the mission, so eager for his success. And his leaders, watching, waiting daily for his return. There could be no success to report now, nothing but failure.

But he had to survive, he had to get back! There could be other missions, but somehow he. had to get back.

The situation fell sharply into his mind, crystal clear. There was no alternative now. He would have to destroy every creature on the ship.

One against seven. He considered the odds swiftly, the sudden urgency of the situation slamming home. They had weapons, the ship was known to them, they could signal for help. There must be *something* to turn to his advantage—

He kicked the alien's foot, thoughtfully—

The lights!

Flicker jumped to his feet, his heart pounding audibly in his throat. Why such brilliant light, why such a slow-cycle current that he could see the intermittent off-and-on? Obviously, what he saw as an oscillation was a steady light to them. With such low light-sensitivity the aliens it have awakened? to have such brilliant lights. They couldn't see without them! The agonizing brilliance that sent Flicker into convulsions was merely the light necessary for them to see at all.

And comfortable seeing-light for him was to them—total darkness!

Far forward in the ship a metal door clanged. Flicker was instantly alert, nerves alive, every muscle tense. Klock was dead, he would be missed by the others. He took a quick glance around him; and removed the weapon from Klock's side, an ordinary, clumsily designed heat pistol, almost unrecognizable, but similar enough to the type of weapon Flicker knew to be serviceable. He strapped it to his side, and moved silently toward the hatchway.

The lights had to go first. Flicker's body ached. His mind was reeling with fatigue, sliding momentarily into hazy attenuation, snapping back with a start. Unless he slept soon, he knew, his reactions would become dangerously slow, and hunger was now tormenting him also. Food and sleep would have to take priority over the lights, no matter how dangerous.

A thought flashed through his mind, and he glanced back at the alien body on the floor. Some of the blood had oozed out on the aluminum floor, forming a dark pool. The thought slid into focus, and the hunger reintensified, into a gnawing knot in his stomach; then he turned away in disgust. He just wasn't that hungry. Not yet.

Quickly he stepped out into the passageway, moving in the direction of the engine sounds. The ship was silent as a tomb except for the distant throbbing of the motors. Far below him he heard the clang of metal on metal, as if a hatch had been slammed. Then dead silence again. No sign that Klock had been missed, not yet. Flicker breathed the cool darkness of the corridor for a moment, and then moved quickly to the ladder at the end of the passageway. His muscles ached, and his neck was cramped, but he felt some degree of his normal agility returning as he peered into the dark hold below, and eased himself down the ladder.

The grainy odor he had smelled above was stronger down here. Halfway to the ceiling the coarsely woven bags were stacked, filling almost every available inch of the hold except for the walkways. A grain freighter! No wonder it had such a small crew for its size. Not many hands were needed to ferry staple food-grains to the aliens on distant planets. Flicker blinked and searched the walkways, finally finding what he wanted—a cubbyhole, behind the stacks, and up against the outer bulkhead. He slid into the narrow space with a sigh, and curled himself up as comfortably as he could. Clearing his mind of every thought but alertness to sound, he sank into untroubled sleep.

He heard the steps on the deck above him, and sat up in the darkness, instantly alert. There were muffled sounds above, then steps on the metal ladder. Abruptly the hold was thrown into brilliant light. Flicker whimpered and twisted with pain as the light exploded into his eyes, and felt a flash of panic as he saw two of the aliens at the bottom of the ladder.

The waves of thought force struck Flicker, heavy with anger and fear. "It couldn't have come far forward in the ship. If Klock was right, that first day, it has a high-order intelligence. It would seek a good hiding place, and then venture out to explore a little at a time. It could be anywhere." The one called Sha-Lee looked back up the ladder anxiously.

The other's mind was a turmoil of jagged peaks and curves. Then his thought cleared abruptly. "But how could it happen? The creature was sedated, almost dead, as far as we could see. It had a shot just an hour before Klock went up there. How *could* it have awakened? And why did Klock go up there in the first place? I thought you left strict orders—"

The two cautiously moved down the walkway. "Whatever happened, it's loose. And there won't be any sedating when we find it again—"

Trembling with pain, Flicker forced his burning eyes to the source of the light in the overhead. He aimed the heat pistol he had taken from Klock, sending a burst of searing energy at the fixture. The hold fell dark as the light exploded into metallic steam.

"He's in here!"

There was a long, pause, in dead silence. Flicker strained to catch the flow of thoughts that streamed from the alien minds.

"I can't see a thing!"

"Neither can I. It got the lights."

They were so near Flicker could almost feel their warmth. Swift and silent as lightning, he sprang up on the grain bags, leaned out just above them. A small bit of wood was near his foot; he grabbed it and threw it with all his might against the far bulkhead. A surge of fear swept from the alien minds at the crash, and they swung and fired wildly. Like a flash Flicker sprang to the deck behind them, pausing the barest instant for breath and balance, then springing quickly forward and striking one of them a crushing blow across the neck. The alien dropped with a small squeak. The other fired wildly, but Flicker was too quick, zig-zagging back to a retreat behind the bags. After a moment he peered over the top of the pile.

Sha-Lee was standing poised, peering into the blackness toward the other alien' who lay quite motionless on the floor, its head twisted at an unnatural angle from its body. Something in Flicker's mind screamed, "Get the other now, while you can!" But he took a deep breath of the sticky air, and then turned and ran silently to the hatch at the back of the hold, and out into the large corridor.

He had to get the lights first. With the lights gone, the others could be taken care of in good time. But he knew that he couldn't stand the torture of the lights much longer; already his eyes felt like sandpaper, and the paralysis which took him for several seconds when

15

the lights first went on could give the aliens a fatal advantage. He, came to a darkened hatchway, half open at the end of the corridor, took a brief inventory, and hurried through. Far below he could hear the generators buzzing, growing stronger and mingling with the sobbing of the motors as he descended ladder after ladder. He hurried down a dimly-lit corridor and tried a hatchway where the noise seemed most intense.

The light from within stabbed at his eyes, blinding him, but he forced himself through the hatch. To the right was the glittering control panel for the atomic pile; to the left were the gauges for the gas storage control. An alien was standing before the main control panel, a larger creature than his brothers, his mind swiftly pulsating, carrying overtones of great physical strength. Flicker slid silently behind one of the generators and studied it and the room, his mind growing progressively, more frantic. His eyes burned furiously, and finally, with a groan, he unstrapped the heat gun and sent a burst toward the ceiling. The light blew with a loud pop, and the alien whirled.

"Who's there?"

Flicker sat tight. The generator he was using for concealment was not functioning probably a standby. Three of them were running in series over to one side, with a fuse-box above them. Flicker's heart pounded. It would have to be quick and sure.

The alien moved swiftly over to the side of the room, and a thin blade of light stabbed out at Flicker. A battle lamp. The suddenness of its appearance startled him, stalled his movement just an instant too long. He saw the burst of red from the alien's weapon, and he screamed out as the scorching energy caught him in the side and doubled him over. In agony he jumped aside and sprang suddenly up onto a catwalk. The alien swung the lamp around below, searching for him, tense, gun poised. In a burst of speed Flicker moved along the catwalk toward the alien, and crouched on the edge directly over him, panting, *gagging* at the smell of the creature mingled with the odor of his own burned flesh. He felt cold rage creep into his mind, recklessness, the age-old instinct of his people to claw and scratch and kill. Suddenly he sprang down past the alien, striking him a light tap on the shoulder as he went by, pinning the creature around like a dervish. The battle lamp went crashing to the deck; the heat gun flew off to one side, struck a bulkhead, and spluttered twice as it shorted out. Flicker spun on the alien, catching him a crippling blow across the chest. Fear broke strong from the alien's mind as he toppled to the floor. Flicker was upon him in an instant, like an animal, ripping, tearing, crushing. The exhilaration roared through his mind like a narcotic, and he lifted the twitching body by the neck, half-dragging it over to the generators. Carefully he placed one of, the alien's paws on one of the generator leads, the other on the other. The terrific voltage sputtered, and the alien gave two jerks and crackled into a steaming, reeking cinder, while the generator turned cherry red, melted, and fused. Flicker blasted the fuse-box with his pistol, fusing it into a glob of molten metal and plastic, then turned the pistol on the auxiliary generators. The smell of ozone rose strongly in the air, and the generators were beyond hope of repair.

Flicker rose and stretched easily, his heart pounding. His side throbbed painfully, but he felt an incongruent flush of satisfaction and well-being. Now there would be no more lights. No more painful, burning agony in his eyes. Now he could take his time—even enjoy himself. He sprang up onto the catwalk again, located a concealed corner, and sank down to sleep.

The five of them were gathered in the control room of the ship. Open paneling of *plastiglass* at the end of the room looked out at the infinity of black starlit space. Far below the engines throbbed, thrusting the ship onward and onward. The aliens moved restlessly, fear and desperation clinging about them like a cloak.

In the darkness of the rear of the control room, high above them on an acceleration cot, crouched Flicker, hunger gnawing at his stomach. He peered down at the flimsy little creatures, studying their features closely for the first time. ShaLee stood with his back to the instrument panel, facing the others, who sat or lounged on the short table-like seats before him. A pair of battle lamps sat on the instrument panel, trained on the two hatchways leading into the control room, and each of the aliens carried a heat pistol in his paw. They looked so weak, so frightened, so utterly helpless, standing there, that it seemed almost impossible for Flicker to believe that these were the creatures who were threatening his people—who were responsible for the draining and pillaging of planets that Flicker had seen. These were the ones, deadly for all their apparent helplessness. Flicker blink ed, leaning closer and closing his eyes, soaking in and separating each thought pattern that reached him from the group.

"So what are we going to do about it?" Sha-Lee's thought came through sharply. "We might be able to manage without the lights, but he got the generators, so that took our radio out too. We got only one message home, and that was brief—not even enough for them to get a fix on us. They know approximately where we are, but they'd never find us in a million years. We can't hope for help from them. We're stuck."

Another one shifted uneasily. "He's out to get us all. And without light we can't find him. We don't even dare go looking for him—it looks as if he can see in the dark."

"Let's consider what we're really up against," said ShaLee. "As you say, he can see in the dark, and we've got darkness here. That's point number one. Number two, he's quiet as a mouse and fast as the -wind. When he got To-may in the grain-storage vault, he came and went so fast I didn't even know what had happened before he was gone. Number three, he's acquainted with spaceships, and with the lights gone he's more at home on this ship than we are. Wherever he came from, he's no primitive. He's got a mind that doesn't miss a trick."

"But what does he want?" Jock toyed with his heat pistol nervously. "What was he doing when we found him out there ? He was nearly frozen to death—"

"—or seemed to be! Motive? It might be anything, or nothing at all. Maybe he's just hateful. The point is, there's one thing he can't do, unless he's *really* got some technology, and that may be our way out."

"Which is?"

"I doubt if he can be in two places at one time. Or three. There are five of us here, and some of us have to get home to tell about this. This could be death to our exploratories. Certainly we don't dare to take him home with us alive, but we'd have to find him to kill him, and he'd get us first. Now here's a plan we might be able to put across. Two of us should stay with the ship, myself and one other. The other three take lifeboats, and get out now. We approach within lifeboat range of Cagli in about an hour. The Caglians won't be happy to see you, but they won't hurt you, and you can bluff your way to a radio. Maybe the two of us here can keep him off until you get help. At any rate, I hope we can."

Flicker lost track of their thoughts as the information integrated in his mind. A chill went through him, driving out even the gnawing hunger for a moment. If they got off in lifeboats, they'd get help, and the mission would really be lost, irreparable damage done. He had to prevent them from making any contact with their home. This ship was a freighter; freighters were slow. Any culture as advanced as theirs would have ships—fast ships—to overtake slow old freighters

Quickly and silently Flicker slipped over toward the hatch. The lamp shown on it full, but the aliens weren't watching. Like a shadow he flashed through the hatch and down the corridor. There he paused, for a fraction of a second, and listened.

No thoughts, no alarm. Flicker felt a wave of contempt. They hadn't even seen him.

At the top of the ladder Flicker crouched and waited. The meeting below was breaking up; he heard a hatchway clang, followed by the muffled pounding of their heavy feet as two of the aliens started down the corridor below. The battle lamp swung back and forth before them, its flash pattern swinging weirdly on the bulkheads and deck. Flicker waited. The aliens started up the ladder before him, their thoughts a muddle, fear oozing from them, but carrying with it a curious overtone of incaution. "We can check the lifeboat for supplies now," came a thought, "and be ready to blast in an hour." At the top of the ladder they passed so close to Flicker that he nearly gagged, yet in his desperate hunger there was something almost tasty—about that smell. They moved on, toward the lifeboat locks, and Flicker followed, trying eagerly to separate their thoughts into a coherent pattern.

"*He's behind us!*" It came suddenly, like a knife through the air.

"Don't turn around." The first alien gripped his companion's sleeve. "Pretend you don't know it." They moved along, with no outward sign of their sudden terrible awareness. Their minds were racing, fearful, but they kept on. Flicker crouched along the bulkhead and followed.

The aliens came to the hatch. Flicker tensed, ready for them. He heard them undog the hatch, heard its squeak as it opened, and he tensed, his muscles quivering eagerly.

Three beams of light stabbed down the passageway at him, brilliant, staggering him LL back against the bulkhead. He grasped frantically at the closing hatch, but it clanged shut, the heavy dogs scraping into place on the opposite side. And at the other end of the corridor

He was trapped! Of course they had been incautious, nonchalant! Of course they had led him on. And now—

"There he is! GET HIM!"

A heat gun whined, its searing energy ricocheting in the closed end of the corridor. With a snarl Flicker sprang, high up on the bulkhead, dragging himself onto a shelf carrying emergency spacesuits. Blast after blast came from the alien guns, rebounding like furies, all missing. "I can't kill it!" a thought pounded through. "It's moving too fast!"

Frantically Flicker trained his own pistol on the hatchway, blasted a steady stream until the metal melted through. With an exultant snarl he dived through the opening, and without pausing sprang up onto the lifeboat locks. He paused, breathing heavily, his burned side throbbing painfully. The two aliens inside were swinging their battle lamp in wild arcs. One spotted him and blasted, but he was gone before the alien triggered. With careful aim he blasted the battle lamp, resting easy for a moment in the ensuing darkness. Then he was across the lock, tearing, ripping, scratching, snarling into the two aliens, roaring in savage glee. One of them fell with a crushed skull, its body horribly mutilated. The other slipped from his grasp and started running through the blackness for the hatch. Flicker was there before it.

He picked up the alien bodily and threw him across the lock. In an instant he was upon him, ripping off an arm at the socket. The alien screamed in pain, and tried to wriggle away. Flicker let him wriggle about three feet. Then he gave him a cuff that sent him sprawling, and ripped off the other arm. The alien twisted and turned like a worm on a stick, but Flicker didn't kill him. Instead, he broke a leg, and twisted off an ear.

The three aliens in the corridor threw open the hatch and flooded the dark lock with the beams of the battle lamps. They saw blood on the deck, and nothing more.

"We know you're in here. Come out now, or we'll come get you." Flicker caught the thought clearly, and snickered comfortably. He was much more comfortable, now that he wasn't so hungry. He picked up a long white bone and threw it against the opposite bulkhead. It clanged, and the three lamps swung instantly in the direction of the sound. "There he is! Blast him!"

Three heat guns spoke sharply, and dead stillness echoed the despairing thought, "That wasn't it—"

They moved across the room, and dragged the charred and mutilated body of their companion away from the bulkhead. "Let's get out of here! We can't fight this thing!" Sha-Lee started for the hatch, followed by the other two.

Only two of the three reached the control room. Flicker played with the third for quite a long while before he killed him.

"We aren't going to get out of this alive," said Sha-Lee. "You know that, as well as I do, I guess."

Jock nodded. "I've been sure of it since he got Klock in the first place. He moves too fast, he thinks too fast, he can see too well. And savage! He has a heat gun, do you realize that? But not One of us was killed with a heat gun. It's butchery, I tell you—no, we won't get out of here, alive."

"And this thing that's stalking us. What will it do? Take the ship back home? Run loose there the way he's run loose here? Killing and maiming? We've got to stop it, Jock. We can't let it get home."

Jock stared at the instrument panel. "I know one way we can stop him," he said slowly. "It's suicide, but it would keep him from going home. And it would mean the end of him, too, finally."

Charlie looked up, tired lines on his face. The fear was gone to resignation now, replaced by another more terrible fear—the fear that they would be killed and leave this thing running loose—on the ship "What is it, Jacques?"

Jacques picked up a space chart, and slowly ripped it in two. "This," he said. "We can cripple the ship, foul up the controls, the gas storage, the charts —cripple it beyond repair. Then he can't do anything! Wreck the engines, destroy the food, smash this ship so no one could ever do anything with it. Completely wreck his chances to get home—"

They moved with sudden desperate swiftness. The heat gun sent up the space charts in wreaths of flame, fused the chart file into a molten heap of aluminum. The engines stopped throbbing, giving way to deathly silence broken only by the heat blasts and the heavy breathing of the two men. The instrument panel melted and exploded, the gas control was smashed. The men worked in a frenzy of fearful destruction, their own last escape going up in searing heat blasts, destruction that no man could even hope to repair, ever

And back in the corner, behind the acceleration cots, Flicker purred and purred. Easy, satisfied contentment filled him for the first time in days; he snickered as the alien creatures went on their path of self-destruction. Everything would be all right now, and his leaders would be pleased at how it turned out. He could bring back first-hand information about these creatures, vital, invaluable information. The contact could be made another time. And then he could go back to his family—they'd really enjoy hearing him tell about that alien, squirming and screeching with both arms ripped off—and have a long, comfortable rest.

The helpless, simple fools! They could kill him so easily, if they only knew. Just a breath of hydrogen, to combine with his high-oxygen metabolism, to explode him like a bomb. But they were destroying everything they could, in a mad, frenzied attempt to stall the spaceship, to keep him out here in space to perish with them! Such a complete job they were doing, and it was so completely and utterly useless.

True, no human being could ever repair those controls to regulate the atomic engines of the ship. No human being could survive the weakening atmosphere long enough to repair the gas units. And even with these repaired and functioning, a human being would be forever stranded in the vast, cold, friendless reaches of space, without a perfect, detailed, visual memory of the space charts easily at his command. For no human being could ever direct a ship blind to a destination, without the charts of the space through which he flew. No human being would ever find his way out of the dead emptiness of such uncharted space.

Flicker curled up and placed his nose gently on his tail, disinterested; unconcerned. A human being would be hopelessly, irreparably doomed out here.

Flicker purred contentedly to himself as he considered the weaknesses of the human race which he had observed. From their view, he was completely stranded.

But a cat can always find its way home.